THE ADVENTURES OF
Katie Bubbles

BOOK 1:

The Boston Adventure

BY STEVEN HILL JR.
ILLUSTRATED BY SYDNEY PATRICIA HILL

For Jeanne,
who always encouraged me to Keep going.

Table of Contents

CHAPTER 1:
Giggles Makes the Mix

It was almost finished. He could see it was almost done. Giggles stirred the weightless floating water-mix in the pool determinedly, ever faster, using his sister, Katie's ping-pong paddle like a giant wooden spoon, proud that he had thought of taking her ping-pong paddle from her closet. His latest invention, his weightless floating water-mix, was coming along great! He kept stirring madly and the mix began to sparkle and shine. As he looked down into the wading pool, the mix seemed to move on its own and Giggles paused. He stirred more slowly and then he stopped stirring all together. He took a long, thoughtful look at the floating water-mix and felt a tinge of fear as he became certain that the mix was moving faster on its own and then an idea hit him. He knew what was needed.

Glug! Glug! Glug! He poured half a bottle of Vermont Maid Maple Syrup into the wading pool to thicken the mix. When the sun came up higher in the sky, things would really start to happen. That's when the mix would warm up and the molecules would get more active than they were now. More maple syrup should keep every-thing from exploding.

A few more stirs and he was done. Time to let things cook, thought Giggles. Giggles tossed the ping-pong paddle on the ground near the wading pool and it banged loudly against some of the empty cans and bottles that he had strewn around while he was making the mix. He jumped at the noise.

Spiders and bugs, he thought. He hoped the noise wouldn't wake up his little sister. The last thing he wanted was his nosy little sister, Katie Bubbles, poking around near his latest invention.

Giggles rubbed his hands together and took a last long look at the mix languishing in his sister's wading pool. "Um," he grunted, "Yes Siree-Sir," he said and gig-gled. Things sure looked good. He turned and barged his way through the empty bottles and cans and opened the back door to the house, neglecting to close it softly behind him. The door clanged shut. Rats! More noise, more of a chance of waking up his sister. He stopped.

Spiders and bugs, he thought. He looked up at the ceiling at the spot just below where Katie's room was. Was that her rustling around up there already? If he had woken her up, then that could lead to trouble. He might even get caught experimenting with science again. The thought of getting caught made him nervous.

Giggles crouched and looked around, fear and apprehension in his eyes. He slouched his way through the mess he had made in the kitchen, feeling guilty as sin. He headed for his room upstairs. Giggles wasn't giggling anymore.

CHAPTER 2:
Katie Bubbles Wakes Up, Smells Trouble and Daydreams a Dream

Katie Bubbles sat up in bed startled. What the heck was that noise? she wondered. It was some sort of banging sound, coming from outside. It was far too early for normal banging noises so Katie knew that this noise had to be trouble. She thought about it a minute. There could only be one explanation for the noise: Giggles. It had to be her big brother, Giggles. Giggles, up to something behind the house near her little pink-on-the outside and blue-on the-inside wading pool, the one that Katie's dad had set up for her in the back yard at the edge of Mom's new patio. Katie sighed. More trouble, more stress. She shook her head. She hoped her smelly big brother hadn't done anything to hurt her new wading pool. She loved having that pool all summer. Katie flopped back on her pillow and closed her eyes and daydreamed about her cool pool.

Katie felt the best part of having a wading pool was when she got to sit in her special little lounge chair and soak her pretty little feet in the warm water. It felt sooooooo good to soak her feet! Sometimes Katie would splash her feet around in the water, and other times she would keep her feet still and stare up into the deep blue sky, listening to the sounds of the rustling leaves and watching the clouds go by.

Katie Bubbles loved watching the big fluffy clouds move slowly across the summer sky. The clouds always changed shape as they silently slipped along in their intricate parade: first monkeys, then chickens, then smiling doggies, then people with big noses and no chins. The clouds were always changing as they glided along on their peaceful way, going who knows where and seeing who knows what.

Sometimes Katie Bubbles wished she could float through the sky like an ever-changing cloud, changing her shape and gliding along, seeing what clouds see and learning what clouds learned wherever it was they went. Wouldn't it be great to glide through the sky and go wherever you wanted to go? Wouldn't that be like a dream come true?

Most people will tell you that dreams seldom come true. Even Katie Bubbles had never had a dream come true. But thanks to her brother, Giggles, very soon, she would!

CHAPTER 3:
Katie Bubbles Goes Outside to See What's Up

Just like all the other boys she knew, Giggles never sat still. He never played quietly, he usually had dirt on him, and sometimes he smelled funny too.

Katie sighed. Daydreaming about clouds had made her feel good, but there was no way to avoid the fact that Giggles had been causing a commotion near her pink-on-the-outside and blue-on-the inside wading pool earlier that morning. Katie decided to go outside to investigate, to see if Giggles had caused any damage to her pool. She pushed her pink satin lightweight cotton blanket aside and hopped out of bed. She went to her bathroom and brushed her teeth, just like her mommy had taught her to do, carefully making sure that each tooth got a little bit of toothpaste on it. Katie was glad that her teeth had finally stopped falling out, because it made her kind of nervous when her teeth fell out. She had worried that she would wind up looking like a scary old witch if her teeth didn't grow back, even though her mom had told her that they would.

Katie Bubbles finished brushing her teeth, rinsed, and spat. She wasn't too good at spitting though. That was one thing her messy brother, Giggles, could do better than she. Katie decided to give each of her front teeth a little tug to make sure that they were stuck firmly in her pink gums. She tugged on the first few. They seemed OK. She didn't want any more teeth falling out; in fact she'd just as soon her teeth stayed where they were forever. She didn't think that having teeth fall out was worth the two quarters the tooth fairy would put under her pillow. Even if the tooth fairy had put five or ten whole dollars under her pillow, Katie would rather have her teeth stay put in her gums; that was for sure.

Katie looked around her room. Almost everything was pink. The walls of Katie Bubbles room were pale pink as was the frilly canopy that her dad had fastened to the ceiling above her bed. Her blanket was satin pink, and the soft rug near her bed that kept her feet from touching the cold hardwood floor in the winter was lavender pink. Katie Bubbles just loved pink.

"Pink," she said, "pink, pink, pink," and the words sounded like music to her, low notes to high. "I love pink," she said, her voice rising up. Katie Bubbles stood still for a minute, lost in her little pink world, and then suddenly she remembered about Giggles and investigating whatever he had been doing out by the wading pool.

Katie Bubbles put on her bubble-gum-pink favorite top and her whiter-than-white sun shorts. She tossed her reddish-pinkish hair (that she secretly wished was brown and thick like her best friend Sujatha Wong-Sanchez's hair) and off she went downstairs. She walked through the family room and saw that the kitchen table was covered with all sorts of bottles, jars, spoons, pliers, toothpaste tubes, wires, and old cell phone and computer parts.

What a mess, thought Katie Bubbles. She shook her head and put her hands on her hips and surveyed the wreckage. She secretly hoped Giggles would get in trouble for making such a gigantic mess. Mom would be mad for sure. Katie Bubbles thought about telling on Giggles and getting her big brother in trouble, and that idea made her feel six feet tall. She smiled slyly and walked on.

Katie was still smiling and thinking about telling on Giggles when she slid the family room sliding doors open, stepped outside, and saw an even bigger mess by the patio and wading pool. There was junk everywhere. Spiders and bugs, she thought. It had to be Giggles making trouble again!

CHAPTER 4:
Katie Bubbles Makes a Bubble

Katie closed the sliding doors and turned and stared at the mess out on the patio. She folded her arms and shook her head. What on earth had Giggle been doing near her precious pool?

She walked over to take a closer look: Bottles and cans, an empty bucket with some green gunk in the bottom, dishwasher powder, Mom's Woolite from down in the basement near the washing machine, Dad's turpentine, a garden hose, three bottles of white vinegar, five rolls of paper towels, duct tape, some big long sheets of tin foil, the empty roll from inside the tin foil with a white coffee filter duct-taped to one end, some olive oil, some mouthwash, a little can of motor oil that Dad used for the lawn mower, some empty hand sanitizer bottles, a can of bug spray, a few jars and tubes of Mom's makeup, some Vermont Maid Maple Syrup, some shoe polish, and some Grecian Formula hair color stuff that Dad called "my shampoo."

Huh! Very weird and very strange, thought Katie. Typical Giggles, typical boy: impossible to figure out and never-ever sits still, my smelly big brother, trouble with a capital T. Trouble walking and trouble talking, living right in the same house with me. It just wasn't fair. Spiders and bugs, Katie thought, having a big brother is almost as bad as living with spiders and bugs.

She walked up to the edge of her pool and peered in and saw water, sparkling and bright. Katie watched fascinated as the water made slow swirls, moving around by itself, shimmering and glistening in the pool on this bright sunny day, the same way the pretty diamond on Mom's wedding ring danced in the light.

Katie cautiously stepped closer to the pool. She looked more closely and was shocked to see her favorite pink Hula-Hoop sitting at the bottom of the wading pool. She knew she hadn't left it there. That sneaky Giggles! Giggles must have taken her Hula-Hoop without even asking her if he could. He was always touching and taking her stuff!

Katie wanted her pink Hula-Hoop out of the weird looking water right away, so she stepped into the wading pool and stood in the center of the Hula-Hoop. She put her hands in the water and grabbed the hoop, one hand on each side, and began to lift the hoop out of the water. She noticed that the water felt thicker and stickier and heavier than water usually felt. She pulled the hoop up out of the water and when the hoop was by Katie's waist, well, that was when Katie saw the bubble forming.

The Hula-Hoop was making a bubble all around Katie, the same way the little hoop on a plastic bubble blower wand makes a bubble when you wave it around. Wow! Katie kept lifting the Hula-Hoop up past her shoulders, amazed as the bubble grew larger and continued to surround her. Katie kept lifting, and the bubble just kept coming, and then suddenly Katie lifted the Hula-Hoop way up over her head and just like that, right in her own back yard, right there at the side of her mom's new patio, Katie Bubbles found herself standing inside a giant shimmering bubble!

CHAPTER 5:
Giggles' Perspective

Giggles Bubbles put his secret physics book down. No one knew he had it. He had found it way in the back of the town library, up in the bell tower, on a day when he was poking around, looking for stuff and checking things out. Giggles was always checking things out and wondering about how things worked because he was really smart. In fact no one knew (or would believe) just how smart Giggles Bubbles really was, especially not his little sister, Katie. Giggles loved his little sister very much, even if she did call him Gigglehead and even if she had to have everything painted pink.

Giggles shifted around on his bed. He had spent the last half hour reading his secret physics book and thinking, waiting for his weightless floating water-mix to heat up in the sun. Now he was kind of tired out, so he was just lying there, thinking about what makes a baseball curve when he heard a splash. Now where did that splash come from?

Suddenly it hit him. The wading pool. His floating water experiment. Katie?

Giggles jumped up and ran over to his window and looked down at the patio from his perch in his upstairs bedroom. He couldn't believe what he saw. Katie was in the wading pool, standing in the middle of his weightless floating water experiment. What on earth was Katie Bubbles doing standing in the middle of his experimental mix? The weightless floating water-mix wasn't ready yet because it needed to absorb more sunlight to generate maximum lifting power. Katie could wreck the whole experiment by standing around in the water-mix and disturbing the delicate molecules.

Spiders and bugs he thought. And rats. He had to get Katie out of the wading pool right away, before she ruined everything.

Giggles ran downstairs, through the kitchen, through the mess he had left in the family room, and threw open the sliding doors; but he was too late. He shook his head in disbelief! Katie was trapped in a bubble, a big giant bubble made from his weightless floating water-mix, the mix that he had been making since the sun first came up early that morning. Giggles was suddenly afraid of what might happen next. He didn't have to wait long to see his worst fears come true.

He rushed forward to help, and then suddenly Giggles Bubbles heard himself shout out, "Katie!" He stopped dead in his tracks watching helplessly as his little sister, Katie Bubbles, rose slowly into the air, encased inside a giant bubble, as weightless as a fluffy cloud floating in an endless blue sky.

CHAPTER 6:
Katie Goes over Sujatha's House

Giggles Bubbles was smart and Giggles Bubbles was fast. The sight of his sister floating away was making him feel crazy. Giggles leapt into action, thinking quickly. He could see Katie slowly ascending into the air above the wading pool, and that made him move even faster because he knew that the bubble formed by the mix would not keep Katie floating forever.

The first thing Giggles did was grab a small, square, empty bottle of Fiji water that he saw on the ground near the wading pool. Giggles quickly filled the empty bottle with some of his weightless floating water-mix, reasoning that Katie might need some more mix later in order to get home.

Then Giggles raced back into the house, bashing through the screens on the sliding doors and bursting into the kitchen. He took a quick glance back at Katie, who was calmly hovering inside the shimmering bubble about six feet above the wading pool. Giggles knew that she would ascend even higher as the bubble absorbed more sunlight, but for now she was floating almost still,

quietly suspended, like a redheaded hummingbird trying to decide what flower to visit next.

As Giggles raced through the family room on his way
upstairs, he grabbed a small quarter-sized disc from
the cluttered kitchen table that was littered with the
electronic gear he had been fidgeting with earlier that
morning. The disc contained a strong signal sender. If
the wind started to blow Katie away, at least Giggles
would be able to track his little sister's whereabouts
on the GPS system he had connected to one of his
many computers.

Next Giggles grabbed two packages of peanut butter and crackers, one package of cheese and crackers,
a box of apple juice, and a chocolate chip granola bar
that he spotted next to his mom's little desk at the end
of the kitchen. Then Giggles ran upstairs to his room.
He grabbed his small backpack and shoved everything
in: the Fiji bottle full of weightless floating water-mix,
the box of apple juice, the quarter-sized disc-shaped
strong signal sender, the chocolate chip granola bar,
and the three packages of crackers: two peanut butter
and one cheese. Everything fit. Giggles raced to the side
window of his room and opened it wide, just in time to
see Katie rise up level with the second floor. Fortunate-
ly the bubble stopped rising, and Katie hovered about
ten feet away from where Giggles was looking out. Her

eyes were wide open with surprise, but she didn't look scared. Not yet.

"Katie," he shouted, "you'll be OK. Take this backpack with you, but don't drink the water, understand?"

Katie nodded her head and said something that Giggles couldn't quite hear, something like, "Thanks a lot, Gigglehead!" and then Giggles took aim and threw the backpack toward the bubble. When the backpack hit the bubble, it made a spongy, wet, smacking sound but, thank heavens, went right through the wall of the bubble and came to rest at Katie's feet—so far, so good.

Giggles started to tell Katie to stay calm, but the sound of rustling leaves diverted his attention; the wind was picking up. Giggles saw the leaves on the trees moving and dancing as the warm summer breeze gained strength. The morning sun was getting stronger. The bubble began to glow and vibrate, shimmering in the sun. Giggles pressed his palms together and bowed his head, but the bubble with Katie in it started to move, and Giggles watched in shock and awe as his sister Katie Bubbles drifted slowly away, drifting steadily over the brightly painted house next door, the house where the beautiful Sujatha Wong-Sanchez lived, the little girl with the wavy brown hair, the smart little girl his sister called "my best friend forever."

CHAPTER 7:
Katie Towers over the Town

Katie Bubbles was feeling scared and uneasy. She was drifting slowly up into the sky, closer and closer to the white fluffy clouds above her, the type of clouds she loved to watch, the ones that forever changed shape. To help herself stay calm, Katie made up a little song that sounded like the Happy Birthday Song. She looked up at the clouds above her and started to sing:

"Well, I'm up in the sky,

But I'm not very high,

And I'm not even falling,

So I won't even cry"

Singing to herself made her feel better so Katie Bubbles made herself focus. She got all of her courage together and looked down. She could see Sujatha's house below her, and that made Katie wonder what it would be like if Sujatha was with her in the bubble. She knew having Sujatha with her would be much more fun than floating alone. But for now she had bigger things to think about.

As Katie gained altitude and floated higher, her attention shifted to the town below. She began to see how the town where she lived was laid out. She could see her own house, and she could see the pizza parlor where Dad always took them for pizza and soda on Saturday nights. Katie could see the town square, the big white church in the middle of the square, and the little grocery store one street over. Katie could see the bell tower on the old town library, where she loved to go to read books and think about how things were and how they came to be.

Katie lived in a beautiful little town not far from the city of Boston. A long time ago—back in the 1600s—a preacher named Philameno Burrow, along with some Pilgrims that had left England to come to America so they could be free from religious persecution, founded her town. Back in England, the Pilgrims had to worship the same way as the English king, but in America they were free to worship any way they wanted, which seemed like a good deal to them, so they got on huge wooden sailing ships and made the dangerous voyage to America, crossing the entire Atlantic Ocean, with not even a single compass or GPS on board to help them find their way and not even a single spark of electricity around to light a single light.

Once he arrived in Boston, Preacher Philameno Burrow saw that Boston was too crowded, and so he decided to

go west and look for a place to build a little town. The only place he could find was a small amount of open space that was right in the middle of four other towns: Eastborough, Westborough, Northborough, and Southborough. So Philameno Burrow founded his town right in the middle of these four other towns, and he called his town Burrowborough after himself, and that was where Katie Bubbles lived, in a quiet house, on a quiet street, in the quiet little hamlet of Burrowborough, not far from the city of Boston.

Katie could see her school now, there at the edge of town. She could even see the next town over, the town of Eastborough. That meant she was heading east and sure enough, as the bubble went even higher, Katie saw the horizon of the city of Boston off in the distance. She could see the Prudential Tower and the Hancock Tower standing high up above the rest of the city, each building more than sixty stories high. Katie pressed her hands and face against the side of the bubble to get a better look at the two tall towers, and that was when Katie discovered that she could steer the bubble by pressing on the side of the bubble in the direction she wanted to go!

Katie knew that there was an amazing, old, and elegant library in Boston. Her dad had taken her there once before. She had asked about a thousand times to go back, but so far no one had taken her. Katie decided to test steering the bubble again. She gave a hard push on the side of the bubble that was facing Boston, and the bubble soared toward Boston, and at a higher rate of speed.

Katie looked backward toward Burrowborough and then forward toward Boston. She paused for a minute and then smiled wickedly. She really wanted to see that library again, and before she could stop herself, Katie Bubbles pushed as hard as she could, and the bubble raced ahead through the clouds, silently speeding toward the heart of the city. The beautiful library that had captured Katie's heart called out to her, and Katie smiled as she sped along safe in her bubble, as free as the clouds in her dreams.

CHAPTER 8:
Giggles Seeks Sujatha's Advice

Giggles stuck his head out the window, took a look, and could not believe his eyes. He was completely horrified and sick with worry. He felt so helpless, watching as his little sister climbed higher into the sky, all the way to the clouds, floating up over the town. He had to do something fast and get her back before his parent's woke up. He clicked the GPS tracker on his Net Book Computer and picked up the signal from the strong signal sender that he had put in the backpack. He could see Katie's position on the map, right over the center of Burrowborough. One thing for sure: he was going to need help getting her back. He took a deep breath and waited for his lightening quick mind to come up with an idea, a plan of action. Yes! That was it. He would run over to Sujatha's house and tell her what happened so the two of them could figure out what to do next, together.

Giggles grabbed the Net Book Computer and headed back downstairs. Sujatha was always up early. He would knock on her door and ask her to help.

It was six a.m. Sujatha was taking care of the altar in the small room at the side of her house. She was carefully dusting the image of Buddha and re-arranging the candles and flowers on the altar so that they were in more pleasing and harmonious positions. She checked that the small bowl for water offerings was full. That was when she heard a loud knock on the kitchen door. Sujatha thought it was strange to hear a knock so early in the morning. She got a feeling that something was wrong. She went to the kitchen door and peeked out. It was Giggles Bubbles, the boy from next door, her best friend Katie Bubbles' big brother. He was all excited and begged her to run out on her deck and look toward the eastern sky, which Sujatha did. What she saw made her blink her eyes to clear them. What she saw didn't seem real, but there in the sky, Sujatha saw her best friend, Katie Bubbles, floating in a giant bubble, slowly moving east toward the city of Boston!

Sujatha knew that this was a time to practice the Buddhist art of mindfulness, the art of moment-to-moment non-judgmental observation, kind of like being in a trance, but awake. By remaining calm Sujatha could avoid getting lost in a tangle of worries about seeing Katie Bubbles floating in the sky. She concentrated and spoke calmly to Giggles, asking him what on earth was going on?

Hearing Sujatha's soothing voice made Giggles feel better. He explained how he had created a weightless floating water-mix in the wading pool, and how Katie had stepped into the mix, wound up in a bubble, and floated away. He told Sujatha that he was tracking Katie on his GPS, and that she was getting closer to Boston. He asked her if she had an ideas about what to do next to rescue Katie, and that was when Sujatha said "Almost-Uncle Dom, call your almost-Uncle Dom," and Giggles started to giggle because it was such a good idea! He couldn't believe he didn't think of it himself, and he ran home to dial the number of almost-Uncle Dom because almost-Uncle Dom could handle any situation.

CHAPTER 9:
Almost-Uncle Dom

Almost Uncle Dom was a man's man. He knew how to do everything that men were supposed to know how to do, and he knew how to do half of the things that women were supposed to know how to do too.

Almost-Uncle Dom could shoot a gun and skin a bear. He could mow grass and change a tire on a truck. He could hammer a nail and go up on a roof and shingle it in a single day. He was an expert car mechanic, an ex-Navy Seal, and he had enough medical training to take care of most minor injuries. He had been a butcher at a kosher deli and a cook at a fast-food restaurant. Once, almost-Uncle Dom had worked for the Boston Police Department as a crime scene investigator. At one time or another he had also worked as an airplane pilot, a podiatrist, a pediatrician's assistant, a pugilist, a para-trooper, an underwater cameraman, a scuba instructor, an archery coach, a ski instructor, a minor league base-ball player, a high school hockey coach, a motorcycle racer, an Episcopalian minister, a pro golfer that once beat Tiger Woods, an amateur wrestler, and a greeter at Wal-Mart. He was a licensed electrician, and he had a college degree in chemistry and another one in math. Almost-Uncle Dom was an expert cross-country skier, a black belt in Tai Chi, and an excellent swimmer. He had run the Boston Marathon three times and he had once climbed Mount Everest. Almost-Uncle Dom was also a fashion expert and an excellent gourmet cook. He could ride horses, fly helicopters, drive a tank, and take a sub-marine down to five hundred feet.

Almost-Uncle Dom had never been a used car sales-man or a politician, and that is why you knew you could trust him to be the kind of guy who could get you out of trouble and home in time for dinner!

He had been dating Katie and Giggle's Aunt Deedee for twelve years now. He came over to Giggles and Ka-tie's house all the time for birthdays and holidays. He was around so much he was like family, and one day Katie had called him almost-Uncle Dom and the name had stuck.

Anyway, almost-Uncle Dom was in his basement lift-ing weights and doing yoga exercises when his cell phone went off. Almost-Uncle Dom picked up his cell phone and saw that it was his almost-nephew, Giggles calling.

Sensing something wrong, almost-Uncle Dom pushed the green button on the cell phone and said, "Hello."

It was Giggles all right and Giggles had one heck of a story to tell!

CHAPTER 10:
Katie Spots Eddie Snivels

Katie Bubbles drifted slowly down toward earth, safe in her bubble—the wonderful, airy bubble created from the scientific mix that Giggles had made in her pink-on-the-outside and blue-on-the inside wading pool. Katie was drifting down toward earth in the vicinity of Boston Common, which was what the people of Boston called the park in the middle of their city. It was so peaceful drifting slowly down among the trees that Katie sighed at the wonder of it all, until she spotted Eddie Snivels lurking behind a tree just where Boston Common turns into Boston Public Garden. There was something about Eddie that just didn't fit with the beauty of Boston Public Garden, and Katie sensed that right away.

Boston Public Garden got its name around 1837. At that time a rich, outdoor-loving businessman named Horace Gray agreed to give thirty acres of his land to the city of Boston on three conditions: First, Horace insisted that the land had to be for the Public and second, Horace insisted that the land be used for a garden.

The third condition was that Horace would get to name this public garden. Horace thought about what to name the public garden for several weeks. During this time he couldn't sleep and he lost fifteen pounds from the pressure of having to come up with a name. Horace had many gifts but imagination was not one of them. In the end, Horace named the public garden, the Boston Public Garden and that is what people still call it today.

Eddie Snivels didn't know that Horace Gray had named the public garden. In fact Eddie Snivels didn't know much of anything. "Don't want too much book stuff stuffed in my head," Eddie would often say. "Stuff in too much book stuff and my head might explode."

Eddie Snivels rubbed his nose with two dirty fingers and then rubbed it again with the back of his sleeve. He coughed and spit on the ground and wiped his lips with both hands. His hands were dirty, but Eddie didn't have any hand sanitizer on him, no sir. He didn't believe in it. "Gotta get used to your own germs," Eddie liked to say.

Eddie Snivels had never worked a day in his life. "If you can't start at the top, then don't start at all" was Eddie's philosophy on work. But he still had to eat and he still had to pay rent, so Eddie thought and he thought about how to make money without having to work for it, and he finally decided to become a dogknapper. That's right, Eddie Snivels stole dogs for a living, mostly little dogs like Yorkies and poodles because they were the easiest to steal, and they couldn't bite too deep either if things went wrong. Dogs that couldn't bite too deep were the best kind of dogs to steal according to Eddie.

On this particular day, with Katie Bubbles silently floating about ten feet above him, Eddie was intently stalking a well-dressed woman that was out walking her pretty little snow-white poodle on a leash through Boston Public Garden. She was about twenty-five yards away and heading right toward Eddie. The poodle's toes were painted pink, and it had a pink ribbon tied on its head like a bow. "Ohhh, it's a pretty one," cooed Eddie. Eddie figured he could sell that dog on eBay for like a thousand bucks, maybe even more! He couldn't wait to get his hands on it.

CHAPTER 11:
Eddie Sees a Ghost
and Katie Saves a Poodle

Eddie's plan was simple, much like Eddie himself. With the scissors he held in his left hand, he would run at the woman, use the scissors to cut the leash, and then scoop up the little dog with his right hand, commanding the woman to "stay still" while shaking the scissors at her to scare her. Oh boy, thought Eddie, gleefully rubbing his dirty hands together, this is gonna be a big day for Eddie Snivels!

The woman drew closer and Eddie got ready to make his move. Eddie took a few running steps toward his victim, grinning from the pleasure of doing his dirty work when all of a sudden he heard a voice cry out from nowhere "Don't run with scissors!" It was Katie of course, shouting down at Eddie from inside her bubble.

Eddie stopped dead in his tracks and looked up. The voice sounded a lot like his poor dead sister's voice, the one that had raised him and the only person in the world that had ever loved him. "Don't run with scissors!" was something Eddie's older sister always told him when he was little, before she got sick and died.

Eddie looked around again but he didn't see anything. He couldn't see Katie because by now the sun had heated the bubble and the bubble was reflecting the light, making the bubble almost totally invisible, so all Eddie could hear was a voice that sounded to him like his dead sister's voice, and all he could see was a blurry, shimmering, round shape hovering above him.

"Put the scissors down," said Katie again. "You could get hurt!"

"Who's there?" said Eddie nervously. "Who is talking to me?" he called out, feeling panic set in.

"It's me, Katie," said Katie Bubbles.

Wouldn't you know it? Everyone called Eddie's poor dead older sister by her initials "KD," for Karen Diane! Eddie felt suddenly dizzy. He sank to his knees on the edge of the pathway. The scissors fell out of his hand and disappeared into the grass. Eddie was frightened out of his wits. He felt suddenly ashamed and guilty. He didn't even care that the woman with the poodle had walked safely out of range.

"I'm sorry KD," said Eddie. "I'm sorry that I was going to steal that little dog."

"You were going to steal a little dog?" said Katie, horrified. "Oh, that is really, really bad," she said. "Stop that right now and never do that again," said Katie.

"OK, KD, OK," said Eddie, rubbing his nose with the back of his hand, starting to sob and cry, "I'll never steal dogs again," he said through his tears. Eddie got up and leaned against a tree, breathing heavily. "Thank you, KD, for setting me straight," he shouted into the air, his voice cracking. "I'll never steal dogs again, I promise," said Eddie. He nervously wiped his nose with his fingers and chewed at his fingernails. "I'll get a job making sandwiches instead!" he cried out, but Katie didn't hear him because the wind picked up and her bubble gained altitude...and just like that Katie was gone.

CHAPTER 12:
Katie Sees a Woman with No Shoes

The wind blew again and the sun slipped behind a fluffy white cloud. The sky got darker, and Katie's bubble settled slowly just above the ground, finally coming to rest by a woman with no shoes. She was half sitting half leaning against a shady tree in the most peaceful part of Boston Common.

Katie studied the woman for a quick minute and then spoke.

"Where are your shoes?" Katie asked the woman from inside the bubble.

The woman without shoes looked up but could not see Katie because the bubble deflected the light. All she heard was Katie's voice, ever so sweet and melodious. The woman was nearly hypnotized by the sound of Katie's soothing voice, so much like the voice of an angel that the woman almost smiled.

"Who's there?" she asked. "Are you an angel?"

"Well, everyone says I am," said Katie Bubbles thoughtfully.

"Can you help me to get shoes, please angel?" asked the woman. "I am so ashamed and depressed to have no shoes. I used to have everything, but then I lost my job and I got sick and my awful husband left, and now I have nothing except this dress. If only I had shoes, I could look for a job and maybe get back on my feet," she said. She looked down and started to sigh. "Can you help me, angel?" she asked, "Please?"

Katie Bubbles hovered in the air and felt a wave of emotions pass through her as she pitied the poor woman who had no shoes. She felt very sad and wanted to help. She wondered if maybe her shoes would fit the woman, and she wiggled her toes a little to test how much her shoes would stretch. That was how she discovered that if she pushed down with her toes, the bubble would descend. Katie wanted to help this woman so she pushed with her toes and the bubble descended to the ground. Surprisingly, as soon as the bubble touched the ground, it broke apart with a soft plop, splattering Katie Bubbles with bubble goo. Katie didn't know it yet but bubble goo deflected light, which made it impossible for people to see her clearly, at least for now.

Katie was standing right next to the sobbing woman and she touched her shoulder and said, "I will help you get some shoes. I don't have any money, but maybe I can get someone to help me buy you some shoes."

The woman felt the touch and heard the voice but saw nothing.

Katie opened up the small backpack that Giggles had thrown to her. She took out the apple juice and the three packages of crackers, two with peanut butter and one with cheese. She gave the two peanut butter packages to the woman and kept the package of cheese and crackers for herself, because cheese was her favorite.

Katie sipped her juice. "How about a little snack while we figure this out?" asked Katie.

All the woman could see was a blurry shape that shimmered in the sunlight. She saw the crackers floating toward her and she took them because she was so very hungry. "Oh, thank you so much, angel," said the woman. She opened the package of crackers and started to eat and the two of them, Katie and the woman with no shoes, sat under the tree, munching their crackers and thinking about a way to get shoes.

CHAPTER 13:
Katie Shops for Shoes and Realizes No One Can See Her

Suddenly Katie had an idea. She finished chewing her cheese and crackers, swallowed politely before speaking, and said, "I have an idea about how to get shoes for you. I'll take a walk on that street over there," and she pointed to a street at the exit to the Public Garden. "That street looks like it will have a lot of shops, and I bet I can find a shoe store there. I'll go in and maybe someone will help me buy shoes, or maybe someone will just give me some shoes for you. Will you mind waiting here until I try my idea and come back?" she asked.

"Oh no," said the woman with no shoes, "I have nowhere to go, so I won't mind waiting for you to come back. Thank you very much for helping me," she said. She smiled at Katie, and then she closed her eyes, leaned back, and wished Katie good luck.

So Katie Bubbles walked off, down the pathway through the Public Garden and all the way to the intersection at the end of the walkway where she waited for the light to turn red so she could cross. A pretty young girl, probably in high school, was standing next to her waiting for the light to change, and Katie pulled at her sleeve and asked her if there was a shoe store nearby; but the girl acted as if Katie wasn't even there and just absent-mindedly brushed at her sleeve where Katie had pulled at it. Katie felt discouraged and looked around at the other people waiting for the light to change. No one was looking in Katie's direction or paying any attention to Katie at all.

The light changed, the walk symbol came on, and Katie crossed the street, careful to walk within the crosswalk. She looked up at the street sign to memorize where she was, and she saw the name of the street was Newbury Street. Newbury Street was a very long, pretty, and very clean street with lots of people all around everywhere. There must have been a hundred shops on this street. There would be a shoe store somewhere on this street for sure.

Katie continued walking and scouting for a shoe store. Someone bumped into her and just kept going. Then another person bumped into her and again just kept going. Katie began to feel mistreated after several more people that were walking along jostled her without saying "excuse me" or even acknowledging that she was there; instead they treated her as if she was invisible.

Invisible. Katie said the word out loud in her head. Invisible. She said it in her head again. Katie was walking more slowly now, thinking about being invisible and suddenly she began to suspect that maybe, just maybe, she was invisible! What if something about the gooey bubble mix that had splattered on her was making her almost impossible to see? What if the drops of mix that spilled on her when the bubble broke were doing something to the light, reflecting it or something? It was really weird. She waved her arms around a little to see if anyone would look her way in order to test her idea. Every once in a while a person would look her way and smile but mostly no one paid any attention to Katie at all. The people that were walking along and talking away on their cell phones paid her no mind. Katie was sure they didn't see her. Neither did the people that were walking along texting and messaging, their fingers flying rapidly over the keys. Katie was invisible to them too. And the people that were rushing along the sidewalk, talking in loud voices to other people? No way could they see Katie Bubbles either. They didn't even know she was there.

In fact the only people that seemed to be able to see Katie were the ones that weren't in a hurry, the ones who smiled, the ones that would let a cell phone ring instead of ignoring the person they were with to answer it. Katie figured that these were the kind of people that knew how to listen, the kind of people that knew how to give their full attention to others.

At last Katie spotted a shoe store. The sign on the store said, Amontillado's Italian Shoes in great big letters. She walked up to the store door, which was mysteriously closed on this warm, sunny day, and she courageously stepped right in. As soon as she walked in she heard a boisterous friendly voice say, "Look at this, a little girl, so pretty like an angel, welcome to my store, little angel. I am Amontillado. But tell me, how come you are here alone my bambina? Where is your mother?"

Katie was on the spot. And right then and there, with no hesitation, Katie Bubbles told a little white lie.

CHAPTER 14:
The Mystery of the Floating Shoes

"Well," said Katie Bubbles, "my mom is in the shop next door. She and I are trying to help a poor woman get new shoes. This poor woman doesn't even have one pair of shoes and this store is full of shoes. Do you think you could give me some shoes for the poor woman that has none, Mr. Amontillado?" she asked.

"Of course not," said Amontillado, "I keep my shoes behind that wall, and I sell my shoes only for money. Unless you have money, you can do nothing but look." Then he coughed...ugh, ugh, ugh. "But I'll tell you what; I'll let you ask my customers if they want to help you in whatever way they wish. One of them might want to help," he said and then he spun on his heels and disappeared behind his wall, and neither Katie nor anyone else ever saw him again.

Katie took a long look around the shoe store. There were three or four women busy trying on shoes. Katie looked them over, hoping to spot the kindest one, and then she took a chance and walked up to an older woman that was sitting, surrounded by beautiful new shoes, trying on pair after pair.

Katie heard the woman tell the sales girl that she was going to buy at least seven pairs of new shoes, and that she wanted nothing but the best Italian shoes in the store. They had to be the very best she said. So Katie wondered if maybe, this woman would be willing to give Katie her old shoes, so that Katie could bring the old shoes to the woman that had no shoes.

Katie went over to the shoe-shopping woman and pointed to her old shoes and said, "Please Ma'am, may I ask you a question? Since you are getting so many pairs of new shoes, do you think I can please have your old shoes so that I can give them to a woman who doesn't even have any?"

The woman turned toward Katie and snapped, "Who's there? I don't have my glasses on, I can barely see you. I can hear your whiny little-girl voice begging though. Stop your begging right now, understand? Stop begging me to give you my old shoes. My answer is No, No, I will not! I will not give my old shoes away to anybody. Tell this woman that has no shoes to get a job and buy her own shoes. I won't help her and I won't give her a single shoe. Let her work for her shoes. Now go away and leave me alone. You are a wretched little girl and you are interfering with the pleasure I get from my shopping. Now go away and do your horrid begging somewhere else!"

The mean words and harsh reprimand hurt Katie's feelings and made her feel helpless. It made Katie sad that the lady wouldn't share her old shoes. It didn't seem fair at all. The mean words the lady had said made Katie so very sad that she choked up and she started to cry and a single tear ran down Katie's cheek. As the tear slid down Katie's cheek, it flowed over a little speck of the bubble mix that had splattered on Katie earlier. The tear mixed with the speck of bubble mix and then it fell off the side of Katie's face and drifted down toward the ground. With a soft splash, the tear landed right on the old shoes that belonged to the Lady that would not share her shoes with anyone.

Katie missed what happened next because she was running out of the store. She needed to get away from the mean lady that had made her cry. So Katie didn't see her tear land on the toes of the old shoes the lady wouldn't share, and Katie didn't see her tear slide down the sides of the shoes. She didn't see the shoes start to vibrate and shake, and she didn't see the shoes start to quiver and quake and slowly rise into the air in the middle of Amontillado's shoe store! The floating water-mix was making the shoes float.

The next thing you knew, the bubble mix on the shoes and the bubble mix on Katie attracted each other like strong magnets, and the shoes rose up and moved through the air, following behind Katie as she hurried out of the store. Katie rushed out the door and the shoes sped along behind her. Katie ran down Newbury Street back toward Boston Common, and the shoes followed her, swirling around in the air behind her, and Katie had no idea.

But All around Katie, people were turning and looking, pointing and laughing, at the mysterious sight of these amazing shoes, floating in the air behind a running little girl. And that is why Katie Bubbles never saw the looks of wonder on the faces of the fashionable people on Newbury St. that had been privileged to witness the miraculous flight of the mean lady's old shoes.

CHAPTER 15:
Katie Finds Herself Alone

Katie found the woman with no shoes just where she had left her, sitting quietly beneath the same leafy tree in the lush Public Garden. Katie didn't know how she was going to tell her about what had happened in the shoe store. She didn't want to make her new friend sad, and she didn't want to be the one to have to explain to her new friend how the mean woman in the shoe store would not give away an old pair of shoes. Katie was still upset about that, still crying just a little, but she knew she would have to explain so she took in a deep breath and just before she started to speak, the woman with no shoes pointed behind Katie and suddenly, excitedly said, "Oh how wonderful, I see you've brought me shoes. Thank you so very much. I can't believe it! You are an angel, aren't you?"

Katie turned to see what on earth the woman was pointing at and that was when she saw the old shoes hovering in the air behind her. She had had no idea the shoes were there behind her, and she had no idea how the shoes got there, but no matter. She quickly grabbed the shoes from the air and handed them to the woman who didn't have any.

"Here," said Katie quickly. "I hope they fit you, and I hope you like them. They are such a pretty color, almost pink but not quite."

The woman took the shoes from Katie's outstretched hand and tried them on. They were a perfect fit. The woman quickly stood up, her pride returning. She took a few quick steps around and around the tree, standing straighter and taller with each step. She soon seemed as tall and as strong as the oak tree beside her.

"Oh, they are sooooo pretty and they fit soooooo well," she said, proudly prancing and posing so that Katie could see how nice the shoes looked on her. "Thank you! Thank you so much," she said.

"You are welcome," said Katie, "I'm glad I could help you. Do you think you will be able to get a job now that you have shoes?" she asked.

"Yes," said the woman. "Now I can go to my interview at the library. You see angel, I am a librarian. I know all about libraries and all about books and now that I have such pretty shoes, I know I can get a job at Boston Public Library. Let me introduce myself," she said, and extended her hand for Katie to shake. "My name is Helen," she said politely, "Helen Andrea."

"And I'm Katie Bubbles," said Katie Bubbles, putting her warm hand into Helen's and shaking hello. "It's nice to meet you."

"And very nice to meet you," continued Helen. "If you ever come to the Library here in Boston, please come by and ask for me. You can also e-mail, text, or phone me. I owe you a favor, and I will be happy to help you any way I can with anything in the library. I better go now though, or else I'll be late for my interview. Thanks again, Katie Bubbles," said Helen, and just like that she slipped into the crowd walking along the main pathway of Boston Common and was gone. Katie was suddenly alone.

CHAPTER 16:
Katie Hears a Roar

Katie looked around. She looked around again, carefully noticing everything in her view. She realized that people were looking at her and not all of them looked nice. She realized that the bubble mix must be wearing off and that she might not be invisible any more, surely not as much as before, and this made Katie feel a little jittery down in her tummy. She decided she better go back in the direction of Newbury Street and go back to the shoe store to see if Mr. Amontillado was still behind his wall; maybe he would let her use his phone. Katie began walking quickly back toward the traffic lights at the corner of Newbury Street. She tagged alongside a tall guy in a blue suit, hoping people would figure that that was her daddy. She didn't look at anyone and kept her head down, and just as she got to the sidewalk, just as she was about to press the button to cross, she heard the sound of a gigantic motor roaring.

What the heck? Katie looked behind her and blinked here eyes. The biggest, reddest monster truck with the biggest wheels she had ever seen came dashing across

Boston Common. The huge truck slammed on its brakes and skidded to a stop about three feet from where she was standing. The floodlights on the truck were flashing, and she could hear someone yelling her name over the loudspeakers attached to the truck. "Katie, Katie, Katie!" Suddenly the driver's door banged open and in a flash out jumped almost-Uncle Dom, dressed in his military fatigues!

"Katie," he said smiling. "Are you OK, angel?" he asked.

Without waiting for an answer, almost-Uncle Dom came around to Katie's side of the truck and gave her a quick hug. He opened the back door of the huge truck with a flourish and lifted her up, and there inside was her best friend, Sujatha, and her big brother, Giggles, calling out "Katie, Katie, Katie," both of them giggling and both of them very happy to see her.

"Get in Katie, get in!" they shouted together and Katie was so excited to see them that she cried and laughed at the same time and almost stumbled as she stepped into the air-conditioned truck. She squiggled into the plush leather seat between Giggles and Sujatha.

"Katie, I knew we would find you! We were tracking you the whole time with my strong signal sender," said Giggles, giggling and snapping his net book shut with a loud click. Katie had no idea what he was talking about, but she said thank you anyway.

Sujatha grabbed Katie's hand and calmly whispered to her, "You're safe now, Katie. We'll be home very soon."

"Yeah, home," giggled Giggles. "Let's go home, Uncle Dom." With a honk of the horn, almost-Uncle Dom put on his siren and pulled away from the curb. As the Boston traffic parted for him, almost-Uncle Dom headed for the turnpike and the short ride back to Burrowborough, with Katie Bubbles and Giggles and Sujatha all as safe as could be, excitedly talking and laughing in the back of almost-Uncle Dom's powerful red monster truck.

CHAPTER 17:
Safe at Home

Katie was back in her room. "Pink," she said out loud. She looked all around at all the shades of pink in her room and decided that the shade of pink on the seat cushion of her rocking chair was closest to the shade of pink on the shoes that had followed her back to where Helen Andrea was waiting. Katie smiled when she thought about how happy Helen Andrea had been to get new shoes, even if they were old.

And now Katie had a new friend at the Boston Public Library. She was sure that having a friend at the library would come in handy some day.

Katie still had the knapsack that Giggles had thrown to her earlier that day when the Bubble had started to float off through the clouds. She opened it. All that was left in there was the quarter-sized plastic-covered disc that Giggles had called a strong signal sender and the square shaped bottle that had once held Fiji water, but was now filled right to the top with Giggles' weightless floating water-mix.

Katie thought about how wonderful it had been to float through the clouds in the floating bubble. She smiled and arched her eyebrows. She knew it would be fun to do that again, especially if Sujatha was with her, so she grabbed the Fiji bottle and opened the door to her closet. She went way to the back, struggling through the boxes of old clothes that her dad had stored there until she came to the funny little door that opened into some storage space that no one knew was there—no one but Katie that is. She opened the door to the secret storage space and placed the bottle inside, next to a picture of her grandma that Katie had hidden there just after her grandma had died.

Katie heard someone knocking on the door to her room. She came out of the closet, stepped into her room, and closed the closet door. She sat at her little desk, folded her hands, and called out, "Come in." The door opened and in walked her giggle-headed brother, Giggles.

"Hey Katie," he said, "Have you seen the Fiji bottle that I threw over to you when you first went in the bubble this morning? It had my weightless floating water-mix in it, and that's the last of the floating water-mix I had. The rest of it in the wading pool all dried up from the sun, and now I can't remember how I made it. I mean I think I can remember, but I didn't write everything down and now...well, anyway Katie, is that bottle still in the knapsack?"

Katie didn't hesitate. She wanted that mix all for herself; no way that she wanted to give it to Giggles. No way at all. "The bottle is not in the backpack Giggle-head," she said slyly but truthfully, like a lawyer in court. "The bottle may have fallen out somewhere in Boston before you and almost-Uncle Dom and Sujatha came to get me. Do you think it's possible it's in almost-Uncle Dom's monster truck?" she asked innocently.

"Who knows," said Giggles. "Spiders and bugs," he said, and he scratched his face and shook his head and walked out of Katie's room, muttering and wringing his hands.

Katie flopped down on her bed. It had been a long day. She looked out at the sky through the skylight in her room. She could see the soft white clouds floating by. It had been so wonderful floating in the sky like a cloud. She wanted to do it again, but next time she didn't want to go alone.

Katie closed her eyes and covered a yawn as sleep approached. She dreamed about the monster truck ride home. During the ride back to Burrowborough, Sujatha and Giggles and almost-Uncle Dom kept asking Katie if she had been scared to float in the sky among the clouds.

"Were you scared, Katie?" they asked. "I bet you were scared, right?" they kept asking.

Over and over, again and again, they asked the same question, a thousand times. "Katie, were you scared?

Were you scared to fly through the sky and float in the clouds?"

And each time they asked, Katie patiently answered in her sweet angel-like voice,

"No, I wasn't scared."

And she really, really meant it.

But nobody believed her.

THE END

Words You May not Know
– Steve's Definitions

PAGE

1:    *Molecules* – Little tiny bits of matter that everything is made of, or so they say.

2:    *Languishing* – If you are all relaxed and comfortable, lying around watching TV, then you are languishing in front of the TV.

     Neglecting – If you neglected to do it...then you didn't do it.

3:    *Apprehension* – When you figure something kind of bad is coming, you feel apprehension.

6:    *Intricate* – Complicated like a jigsaw puzzle when it first comes out of the box.

7:    *Commotion* – a noisy, loud, messy state of affairs. "There was a big commotion in the line for free ice-cream"!

10:    *Surveyed* – If you surveyed it, then you looked it over pretty good.

12:    *Shimmering* – Brightly shining and shaking or vibrating, all at the same time.

15:    *Perspective* – This just means viewpoint or how a person looks at things. "I have my own perspective on that."

Physics – The study of the how things work, things like gravity, sound waves and light. Physics is a little bit of Math and a lot of common sense, the way I see it.

18: *Reasoning* – This is when you think things out, in a step 1, step 2, step 3 fashion, without a lot of emotion involved.

Absorbed – Something is absorbed when it gets soaked up. Think of a paper towel soaking up spilled water.

19: *Suspended* – Stuck in the middle of the air. If I am hanging on a tree limb, I am suspended in the air.

Fidgeting – If you are fidgeting with something, you are fooling around with it.

21: *Diverted* – Kind of like a detour...something that makes you go in another direction. A distraction.

22: *Focus* – Paying close attention to something, keeping only one thing in your mind. "Focus on your homework. Focus on the soccer ball."

23: *Altitude* – The amount of sky above you. If you are in an airplane then you gain altitude when you take off and lose altitude when you land.

Persecution – When someone picks on you, you are suffering persecution.

Founded – If you founded it, then you are the guy or woman that started it.

Worship – When you go to Churches or Synagogues or Mosques or Temples and give praise to God, you are worshiping.

25: *Hamlet* – Like a little village. A hamlet is what they called small towns in the old days.

Elegant – Beautiful and graceful.

28: *Buddha* – A regular guy from India that sat under a tree and figured out a whole lot about life and what life means. A great teacher and a man of wisdom, respected all over the world.

Harmonious – When everything fits together and everything is going good, then things are harmonious. This word is based on the musical term, harmony.

31: *Kosher* – This is the word for Jewish laws about food preparation. If food is kosher, then it is fit to eat. People often use the word more commonly though. If things are kosher, then things are all good!

Podiatrist – Foot Doctor.

Pugilist – This is an old word that means a boxer or fighter.

Pediatrician – A doctor that specializes in kids.

32: *Tai Chi* – A Chinese Martial Art based on circular movements. Also a system of movements that promote health.

Gourmet – If you are a gourmet, then you know all about food, the best foods and how to cook them. Probably you like to eat. Gourmets never eat fast food.

33: *Vicinity* – in the area of or neighborhood of.

34: *Philosophy* – your viewpoint, the way you look at it, is your philosophy.

41: *Deflected* – It something deflects something, it means it bounces off of it.

Melodious – Music that is pleasing is melodious. The word is based on the musical term "melody". The melody of the song is the way you sing it, the tune.

45: *Discouraged* – When you feel like giving up, you are discouraged.

Acknowledging – If you acknowledge something, you give a sign you are aware of it. If I acknowledge you are sick, I might say, "hey, do you have a cold"?

Jostled – accidental bumping or shoving.

47: *Boisterous* – Loud and friendly, noisy but nice.

Bambina – An Italian word for "pretty little girl."

50: *Wretched* – Awful, horrible.

Reprimand – When someone tells you what to do in a mean sort of way, it's a reprimand.

52: *Privileged* – Honored, given an opportunity to see or do something special.

55: *Prancing* – Sort of dancing around and showing off a little.

Made in the USA
Las Vegas, NV
11 December 2022

61840500R00044